DATE DUE		
15 SEP '97			
22 SEP. 1999			
2 1 OCT. 1999			
15 SEP 00			
01 OCT '01			
22 SEP '02			
30 MAI '03			
17 JUIN '0A			

STARRING FIRST GRADE

Story by
Miriam Cohen

Pictures by
Lillian Hoban

A Young Yearling Book

Published by
Dell Publishing Co., Inc.
1 Dag Hammarskjold Plaza
New York, New York 10017

Printed in the United States of America

September 1987

10 9 8 7 6 5 4 3 2 1

W

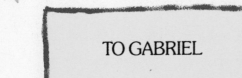

TO GABRIEL

"First Grade has been asked to put on a play for the school," the teacher said. "Which story should we do?"

Everybody wanted "The Three Billy Goats Gruff," especially Danny. He said, "I want to be the biggest goat that knocks off the troll's ears!"

The teacher picked Paul to be the troll, and Danny to be the biggest billy goat. She picked Sara and Margaret to be the other two goats. "We will have to make up more parts so everyone can be in the play," she said.

Anna Maria said, "We could have a little girl snowflake that dances. I'm the only one that knows how to do it, because we have snowflakes at my dancing class."

Danny said, "No snowflakes!"
But the teacher said Anna Maria could be one.

"We need some trees to stand by the bridge," said the teacher. "Jim, you'd make a good, strong tree. And George, and Louie, and Willy, and Sammy too."

"Well, somebody has got to be the trees," Willy said to Sammy.

But Jim didn't want to be a tree. He wanted to be the troll and make awful faces and scare everybody. He wanted to shout, "Who is going over *my* bridge?"

They began to rehearse. Suddenly, the tree that was Jim started singing, "This Land Is Your Land."

"A singing tree! That's stupid," Anna Maria said.

Paul was mad. "He's interrupting me!" he complained.

"It's not like you to act this way, Jim," the teacher said.

Jim didn't sing anymore, but he began telling the others what to do. And he kept telling Paul how to be the troll.

"Make him be quiet!" Paul shouted.

Finally, the teacher said, "Jim, go and sit down."

Jim began talking to himself. "I might not even be here for the play. I'll probably be going to Disney World."

Anna Maria heard him. She said, "You're just making that up."

"You don't know what my father said!" Jim shouted.

The teacher came over. "Jim, how would you like to be the river that goes under the troll's bridge? You could hide under this blue cloth and move around so it looks like water."

Jim stayed under the cloth and stopped bothering the other actors. But Paul was still mad at him.

After school, Paul said, "You think you're the boss of everybody!"

He didn't talk to Jim for a whole week, not even on Friday, the day of the play.

On Friday the school band played as hard as it could. All the classes marched in.

Soon the auditorium was full of people waiting for the play to begin. The principal made a long speech about the play.

Backstage, the teacher whispered,

"Get ready, First Grade. The curtain is going up in one minute!"

Then the curtain went up. On the bright stage, the troll waited under the bridge. The trees were in their places.

The snowflake twirled about near the river.

Sara started across the bridge, Trip-trop, trip-trop.
But Paul didn't say anything. He just stared at
the lights and people.

The teacher whispered, "Who is going across my bridge?" But Paul just stared and stared.

"He's got stage fright," the people said to each other. It was awful! Nobody could think what to do.

Then the river lumped up and said, "Somebody is going over your bridge, Mr. Troll. They are going trip-trop, trip-trop."

"Yes!" shouted Paul. "Somebody _is_ going across my bridge and they better watch out! I'll eat them up!" Then they all did their parts perfectly.

At the end, Danny caught the troll and knocked off his ears.

Everybody cheered for First Grade.

heir teacher pushed Jim and Paul in front for
bow.

And they grinned and grinned at each other.